Dear Parents:

Congratulations! Your child is taking the first steps on an exciting journey. The destination? Independent reading!

STEP INTO READING® will help your child get there. The program offers five steps to reading success. Each step includes fun stories and colorful art or photographs. In addition to original fiction and books with favorite characters, there are Step into Reading Non-Fiction Readers, Phonics Readers and Boxed Sets, Sticker Readers, and Comic Readers—a complete literacy program with something to interest every child.

Learning to Read, Step by Step!

Ready to Read   Preschool–Kindergarten
• big type and easy words • rhyme and rhythm • picture clues
For children who know the alphabet and are eager to begin reading.

Reading with Help   Preschool–Grade 1
• basic vocabulary • short sentences • simple stories
For children who recognize familiar words and sound out new words with help.

Reading on Your Own   Grades 1–3
• engaging characters • easy-to-follow plots • popular topics
For children who are ready to read on their own.

Reading Paragraphs   Grades 2–3
• challenging vocabulary • short paragraphs • exciting stories
For newly independent readers who read simple sentences with confidence.

Ready for Chapters   Grades 2–4
• chapters • longer paragraphs • full-color art
For children who want to take the plunge into chapter books but still like colorful pictures.

STEP INTO READING® is designed to give every child a successful reading experience. The grade levels are only guides; children will progress through the steps at their own speed, developing confidence in their reading.

Remember, a lifetime love of reading starts with a single step!

Special thanks to Venetia Davie, Ryan Ferguson, Charnita Belcher, Tanya Mann, Julia Phelps, Sharon Woloszyk, Nicole Corse, Rita Lichtwardt, Carla Alford, Renata Marchand, Michelle Cogan, Julia Pistor, Rainmaker Entertainment and Patricia Atchison and Zeke Norton

Published in the United States by Random House Children's Books, a division of Penguin Random House LLC, 1745 Broadway, New York, NY 10019, and in Canada by Random House of Canada, a division of Penguin Random House Ltd., Toronto.

Step into Reading, Random House, and the Random House colophon are registered trademarks of Penguin Random House LLC.

Visit us on the Web!
StepIntoReading.com
randomhousekids.com

Educators and librarians, for a variety of teaching tools, visit us at RHTeachersLibrarians.com

ISBN 978-0-553-52438-3 (trade) — ISBN 978-0-553-52439-0 (lib. bdg.) — ISBN 978-0-553-52440-6 (ebook)

Printed in the United States of America
10 9 8 7 6 5 4 3 2 1

Adapted by Devin Ann Wooster

Based on the screenplay by Marsha Griffin

Illustrated by Ulkutay Design Group

Random House 🏠 New York

Courtney is a princess.
Oops! She goes to a camp
for pop stars by mistake!

Erika is a
pop star. Uh-oh!
She goes to a camp
for royals by mistake!

Courtney goes to class
with the pop stars.
She is shy.
She tries singing.

Erika goes to class
with royal campers.
She takes care
of a unicorn!

Courtney dresses up
like a rock star.
She has fun.
She makes new friends.

Erika sings.

The royals like her voice.

She makes new friends,
too.

Lady Anne runs
Camp Royalty.
Finn runs Camp Pop.
They do not get along.
They each want the other
camp to close.

They decide to have
a singing contest.
The losing camp
will close.

Clive works for
Camp Royalty.
Erika hears him
on the phone.

Clive will pay a judge
to make Camp Royalty
the winner.
Clive is cheating!

Erika meets Courtney.

Erika likes Camp Royalty.

Courtney likes Camp Pop.

Erika tells Courtney
that Clive is cheating.
Erika and Courtney decide
to save both camps.

Courtney practices
with the pop stars.

Erika practices

with the royal campers.

It is time for the show!

Camp Royalty sings first.

Camp Pop joins the show.

Together, they are great.

Courtney and Erika
work together.
They are really good!
Everyone loves the show.

Courtney is happy.

She feels brave.

Erika is happy.

She has new friends.

Who is the winner?

Camp Royalty!

Finn and Lady Anne

become friends.

They change the rules.

Both camps win the contest!

They will become one camp.

Courtney and Erika
cannot wait
for camp next summer!